Hunnypot  Library

Winnie-the-Pooh

Tigger Has Breakfast

Adapted from the stories by A.A. Milne

Winnie-the-Pooh woke up suddenly in the middle of the night and listened. He got out of bed, lit his candle, and went to see if anybody was trying to get into his honey-cupboard. They weren't so he got back into bed. Then he heard the noise again.

"Is that you, Piglet?" he said.

But it wasn't.

The noise went on.

"*Worraworraworraworraworra*," it said.

"There are lots of noises in the Forest, but this is different," thought Pooh. "It isn't a growl, and it isn't a purr, but it's a noise of some kind, made by a strange animal! I shall get up and ask him not to do it."

He got out of bed and opened his front door.

"Hallo!" said Pooh.

"Hallo!" said Whatever-it-was.

"Who is it?" Pooh asked.

"Me," said the strange voice.

In the candle-light, Whatever-it-was and Pooh looked at each other.

"I'm Pooh," said Pooh.

"I'm Tigger," said Tigger.

Pooh had never seen an animal like this before. "Does Christopher Robin know about you?"

"Of course he does," said Tigger.

"Well," said Pooh, "it's the middle of the night which is a good time for going to sleep. Tomorrow morning we'll have some honey for breakfast. Do Tiggers like honey?"

"They like everything," said Tigger cheerfully.

"Then if they like going to sleep on the floor, I'll go back to bed," said Pooh, "and we'll do things in the morning. Good night."

And he got back into bed and went fast asleep.

In the morning, the first thing Pooh saw was Tigger, sitting in front of the mirror, looking at himself.

"I've found somebody just like me. I thought I was the only one of them," said Tigger.

Pooh began to explain what a mirror was, but just as he was getting to the interesting part, Tigger said:

"Excuse me a moment, but there's something climbing up your table," and with one loud "*Worraworraworraworraworra*" he leapt up and pulled the tablecloth to the ground. After a terrible struggle, he said: "Have I won?"

"That's my tablecloth," said Pooh, as he began to unwind Tigger.

"I wondered what it was," said Tigger.

"It goes on the table and you put things on it."

"Then why did it try to bite me when I wasn't looking?"

"It didn't," said Pooh.

Pooh put the cloth back on the table, placed a honey-pot on the cloth, and they sat down to breakfast.

Tigger took a large mouthful of honey. He looked up at the ceiling with his head on one side, and made exploring noises with his tongue...and then he said:

"Tiggers don't like honey."

"Oh!" said Pooh, trying to sound sad. Pooh felt rather pleased about this, and said that when he had finished his own breakfast, he would take Tigger round to Piglet's house, and Tigger could try some haycorns.

"Thank you, Pooh, because haycorns are really what Tiggers like best."

Off they set and Pooh explained as they went that Piglet was a Very Small Animal who didn't like bouncing, and asked Tigger not to be too Bouncy at first.

Tigger said that Tiggers were only bouncy before breakfast, and that as soon as they had had a few haycorns they became Quiet and Refined.

They knocked on the door of Piglet's house.

"Hallo, Piglet. This is Tigger."

"Oh, is it?" said Piglet. "I thought Tiggers were smaller than that."

"Not the big ones," said Tigger.

"They like haycorns," said Pooh, "so that's what we've come for, because poor Tigger hasn't had any breakfast yet."

"Help yourself," said Piglet.

After a long munching noise Tigger said:

"Ee-ers o i a-ors."

Then he said: "Skoos ee," and went outside.

When he came back in he said: "Tiggers don't like haycorns."

"But you said they liked everything except honey," said Pooh.

"Everything except honey *and* haycorns," explained Tigger.

Piglet, who was rather glad that Tiggers didn't like haycorns, said, "What about thistles?"

"Thistles," said Tigger, "are what Tiggers like best."

So the three of them set off to find Eeyore.

"Hallo, Eeyore!" said Pooh. "This is Tigger."

"What is?" said Eeyore.

"This," explained Pooh and Piglet together. Tigger smiled.

"He's just come," explained Piglet.

Eeyore thought for a long time and then said: "When is he going?"

Pooh explained that Tigger was a great friend of Christopher Robin's, who had come to stay in the Forest; and Piglet explained to Tigger that he mustn't mind what Eeyore said because he was *always* gloomy; and Tigger explained to anybody who was listening that he hadn't had any breakfast yet.

"I knew there was something," said Pooh. "That was why we came to see you, Eeyore."

"Then come this way, Tigger," said Eeyore.

Eeyore led the way to a patch of thistles, and waved a hoof at it.

"A little patch I was keeping for my birthday," he said, "but what *are* birthdays? Help yourself, Tigger."

Tigger thanked him and looked at Pooh.

"Are these really thistles?" he whispered.

"Yes," said Pooh.

"What Tiggers like best?"

"That's right," said Pooh.

So Tigger took a large mouthful, and he gave a large crunch.

"*Ow!*" said Tigger.

He sat down and put his paw in his mouth.

"What's the matter?" asked Pooh.

"*Hot!*" mumbled Tigger.

He stopped shaking his head to get the prickles out, and explained that Tiggers didn't like thistles.

"But you *said* that Tiggers liked everything except honey and haycorns," said Pooh.

"*And* thistles," said Tigger, who was now running round in circles with his tongue hanging out.

Pooh looked at him sadly.

"What are we going to do?" he asked Piglet.

Piglet said at once that they must go and see Christopher Robin.

"You'll find him with Kanga," said Eeyore. He came close to Pooh, and said in a loud whisper:

"*Could* you ask your friend to do his exercises somewhere else? I shall be having lunch directly, and don't want it bounced on just before I begin. A trifling matter but we all have our little ways."

Pooh called to Tigger.

"Come along and we'll go and see Kanga. She's sure to have lots of breakfast for you."

Tigger rushed off, excitedly.

As Pooh and Piglet walked after him, Pooh thought of a poem:

What shall we do about
poor little Tigger?
If he never eats nothing
he'll never get bigger.
He doesn't like honey and
haycorns and thistles
Because of the taste and
because of the bristles.
And all the good things
which an animal likes
Have the wrong sort of swallow
or too many spikes.

"He's quite big enough anyhow," said Piglet.

Pooh thought about this, and then he murmured to himself:

> *But whatever his weight in pounds,*
> *shillings, and ounces,*
> *He always seems bigger because*
> *of his bounces.*

"And that's the poem," said Pooh. "Do you like it?"

"All except the shillings," said Piglet. "They oughtn't to be there."

"They wanted to come in after the pounds," explained Pooh, "so I let them. It is the best way to write poetry."

At last they came to Kanga's house, and there was Christopher Robin.

"Oh, there you are, Tigger!" said Christopher Robin. "I knew you'd be somewhere."

"I've been finding things in the Forest," said Tigger importantly. "I've found a pooh and a piglet and an eeyore, but I can't find any breakfast."

Pooh and Piglet explained what had happened.

"Don't *you* know what Tiggers like?" asked Pooh.

"I expect if I thought very hard I should," said Christopher Robin, "but I *thought* Tigger knew."

So they went into Kanga's house. They told Kanga what they wanted, and Kanga said very kindly, "Well, look in my cupboard, Tigger dear, and see what you'd like."

She knew at once that, however big Tigger seemed to be, he wanted as much kindness as Roo.

"Shall I look, too?" said Pooh, who was beginning to feel a little eleven o'clockish. And he found a small tin of condensed milk (that he thought Tiggers wouldn't like) and took it into a corner by itself.

But the more Tigger put his nose into this and his paw into that, the more things he found which Tiggers didn't like.

And when he had found everything in the cupboard, and couldn't eat any of it, he said to Kanga, "What happens now?"

But Kanga and Christopher Robin and Piglet were all watching Roo have his Extract of Malt. And Kanga was saying, "Now, Roo dear, you promised."

"What is it?" whispered Tigger to Piglet.

"His Strengthening Medicine," said Piglet. "He hates it."

So Tigger came closer, and he leant over the back of Roo's chair.

Then suddenly he put out his tongue, and took one large galollop, which made Kanga jump with surprise. "Oh!" she said, and then clutched at the spoon just as it was disappearing, and pulled it safely back out of Tigger's mouth. But the Extract of Malt had gone.

"He's taken my medicine, he's taken my medicine!" sang Roo happily.

Then Tigger looked up at the ceiling, and closed his eyes, and his tongue went round his chops, in case he had left any outside, and a peaceful smile came over his face as he said, "So *that's* what Tiggers like!"

Which explains why he always lived at Kanga's house afterwards, and had Extract of Malt for breakfast, dinner, and tea. And sometimes, when Kanga thought he wanted strengthening, he had a spoonful or two of Roo's breakfast after meals as medicine.

"But *I* think," said Piglet to Pooh, "that he's been strengthened quite enough."